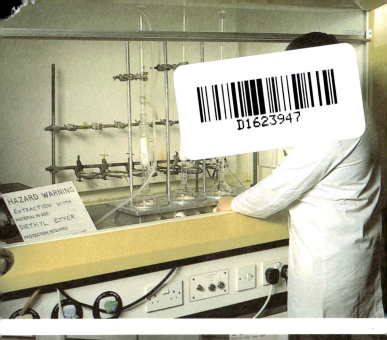

Children don't need expensive chemistry sets or dangerous chemicals to begin to explore sound scientific principles.

This book presents chemistry as it affects our daily lives and, using household items, encourages children to make scientific investigations and observations. The experiments are fun — from sugar crystals to moving mothballs, and baking to growing crystal gardens.

Acknowledgments

The author and publishers would like to thank the following for extra material used in this book. Page 7 (bottom), Pilkington Brothers Ltd; pages 16 and 30, Popperfoto; pages 18 and 50, Alan Hutchison Library; pages 21 and 48, G I Bernard and Dr J A L Cooke, Oxford Scientific Films; page 23 (top), John Paull; page 34, The Wiggins Teape Group Ltd; page 49, Smith and Nephew Pharmaceuticals Ltd; and for their co-operation in the taking of photographs for the front endpaper and page 6 (top), Fisons Pharmaceuticals Ltd, Loughborough.

First Edition

© LADYBIRD BOOKS LTD MCMLXXXII

Simple
Chemistry

written by JOHN and DOROTHY PAULL
illustrations by PETER ROBINSON
photographs by TIM CLARK

Ladybird Books Loughborough

The beginning of chemistry

Chemistry is not a new science. Just when it started, nobody quite knows because its history is clouded by the mists of time. Medieval artists have pictured the first chemists as wizened old men stirring mixtures of bats' brains, frogs' eyes, and lizards' tongues in bubbling cauldrons, muttering strange and peculiar spells.

The first chemists were called *alchemists*. The word *alchemy* means the ancient art of trying to change ordinary metals into gold. About six thousand years ago, some priests discovered how to produce gold by melting gold ore. They also made medicines from herbs and roots of plants which they gathered in the forests. In 1144 AD, Robert of Chester revealed the priests' secrets when he published many of their recipes and their instructions on how to make gold. Alchemy became very popular as people experimented with the ideas in Robert's book. Soon almost every village had its own alchemist, often an eccentric old person living alone, convinced he or she could perform magic.

These people relied on superstitions and sold concoctions to cure all kinds of ailments, from warts to bad wounds. They also made poisons from plants, to kill vermin that destroyed crops. They wrote and sold spells to improve the harvest, and bottled mysterious potions that promised eternal youth to the drinker.

It wasn't just the common folk who believed in the alchemist. Even Queen Elizabeth I had a full time alchemist in her court — but he couldn't have been very successful because the records show that he ended up in the Tower of London. Much of the intrigue and 'hocus-pocus' of the alchemists' work disappeared when Robert Boyle (1627-1691), a British physicist and chemist, concentrated on developing medicines and pills for the sick, beginning the traditions of the modern chemist.

An alchemist at work

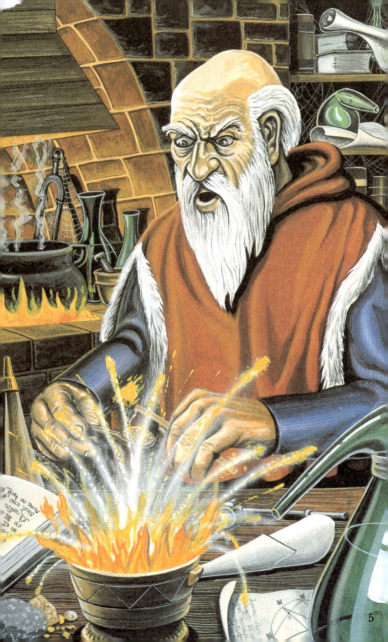

Chemists today

Today there is a chemist's shop in almost every High Street in our towns and villages. They are run by *pharmaceutical* chemists, (the word pharmaceutical comes from a Greek word meaning drugs), who dispense medicines and pills prescribed by doctors to their patients. They no longer make many medicines as most are prepared on a big scale by large drug companies.

In industry there are chemists who spend their working time doing research. They have changed our daily lives by using natural and man-made materials to produce new medicines, agricultural materials and clothing fabrics. Working with doctors, farmers and industrialists, chemists help us to live healthier and more comfortable lives.

Every day we use many materials produced as a result of a *chemical change*. This means that a new substance is made through the action of one material on another. Steel is produced when iron ore is heated in huge furnaces; glass is created from sand that is heated until it melts. Other chemically produced substances are detergents, plastics and rubber.

In this book we are going to explore some household chemical substances. You don't need many special items for the experiments because you can probably find them in your kitchen at home.

PLEASE REMEMBER TO ALWAYS ASK A GROWN-UP FOR PERMISSION BEFORE TAKING THINGS FROM THE KITCHEN.

Chemists, like all scientists, always write notes about their experiments. You could keep a record of all your investigations. Remember to read the instructions and to follow them carefully.

top *Bottles being filled with multi vitamin pills*

bottom *A sheet of glass comes off a production line*

Equipment for your chemistry laboratory

Here is a list of some of the equipment you need for the experiments in this book. When you decide to try an experiment, collect all the things you need, cover a working top or table with newspaper, and place everything needed for the experiment in front of you. Don't get half way through an investigation and find that something is missing. You may ruin an experiment by going to search for something at a vital time.

Containers:
(Collect as many as you can. Wash and dry them, and keep them safe until you need them.)

old cups and saucers,
metal foil dishes,
liquid detergent containers,
clean yogurt pots,
milk bottle tops,
old saucepans, plastic bags,
heat-proof Pyrex jug,

small glass jars with lids
(e.g., meat or fish paste jars),
egg cups,
jam jars of various sizes,
plastic bowl or bucket,
sieve, matchboxes

Some of the substances you will need:
sugar, salt, alum,
cream of tartar,
baking powder,
beetroot, red cabbage,
washing soda
(sodium carbonate crystals),

vinegar, tea leaves,
coffee, earth,
soap powder or detergent,
garden lime,
sand, onion skins

Other items:
magnifying glass,
cardboard,
matches, string,
nylon thread,
tablespoons,
teaspoons,

cotton wool,
paper, tissues,
notebook and pencil,
tapers or spills,
drinking straws,
scissors,
paper towels or kitchen roll

Testing things

Chemists study many different substances in their laboratories and find out what they can about them. When they are given an unknown substance, they first look at it closely to see if they can recognise it. If they can't, they experiment on the unidentified substance with other chemicals and watch what happens. These other chemicals are known as *testing agents*.

We can learn more about ordinary everyday substances in the same way. Our testing agent is vinegar, which is a weak acid (usually ethanoic acid). When an acid like vinegar comes into contact with certain substances, fizzy bubbles are produced. These bubbles are a gas called *carbon dioxide*. Let's find out how many substances in your kitchen produce carbon dioxide bubbles.

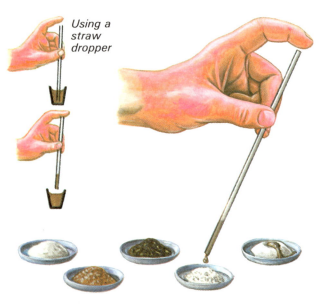

Using a straw dropper

Release a few drops of vinegar onto each substance

Things you need for this experiment:

1 eggcupful vinegar

1 teaspoonful each of: starch,
  salt,
  sugar,
  baking powder,
  tea leaves,
  coffee,
  soap powder
  (or detergent)

1 Alka Seltzer tablet
10 clean, dry, milk bottle tops
drinking straw
drinking glass

What you do:

(1) Put the milk bottle tops in front of you and carefully place a small amount of each powder to be tested into separate milk bottle tops. Leave the Alka Seltzer tablet until later.

(2) Use the straw as a chemical dropper. Dip one end of the straw in vinegar and place one finger over the end as you take it up from the liquid. Drops of vinegar can be released by removing the finger at the top of the straw. Put one or two drops of vinegar onto each different substance in the milk bottle tops.

(3) Watch each one carefully and make a note of what happens. If the vinegar makes each substance fizz, carbon dioxide gas is being produced.

(4) Now put the Alka Seltzer tablet into a glass of water. What happens? You should see the tablet sink to the bottom and produce a stream of carbon dioxide bubbles. In scientific terms, even cold water is warm, compared to ice for example. If you hold the bottom of the glass, you will feel the cold water get colder. The reaction of the tablet and the production of carbon dioxide takes heat from the water, cooling the liquid down.

The moving moth balls experiment

Things you will need:

a large jam jar
moth balls
   (obtainable from a chemist
   or hardware store)

water
tablespoon
baking soda
vinegar

What you do:

(1) Pour some cold water in the jar until it is about three-quarters full and add a tablespoonful of baking soda and a tablespoonful of vinegar.

(2) Stir the mixture well until all the baking soda has disappeared. Let this mixture settle.

(3) Put some moth balls into the solution.

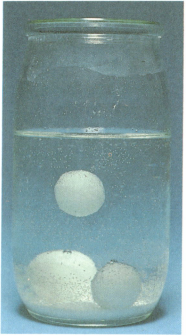

(4) They sink to the bottom but after several minutes you will see bubbles of carbon dioxide form around them and the moth balls will rise to the surface. The bubbles burst as they come into contact with the air, and the moth balls sink to the bottom of the jar. More carbon dioxide bubbles form and the moth balls rise again.

Carbon dioxide bubbles are formed and the mothballs rise to the surface

What is carbon dioxide?

Carbon dioxide is an invisible gas present in the air. When we breathe out, carbon dioxide comes out from our lungs. If we separate carbon dioxide from all other gases in our atmosphere, we find that it amounts to about one part for every three and a half thousand parts of air.

You can see the effect of the carbon dioxide gas we breathe out in the following experiment. You need a teaspoonful of garden lime such as gardeners use in the winter months to condition garden soil. (*Be sure to wash your hands after using lime because it can irritate the skin.*)

What you do:

(1) Put the lime into a jar and half fill with tap water.

(2) Stir it well and let it stand until it has settled.

(3) Pour off the liquid into another jar, leaving the lime sediment at the bottom. You can throw this away as it isn't needed anymore.

(4) Blow gently into the liquid through a straw.

What happens? The liquid turns cloudy because the carbon dioxide gas in your breath joins with the lime water to make a substance called *calcium carbonate*, which turns the water a milky colour.

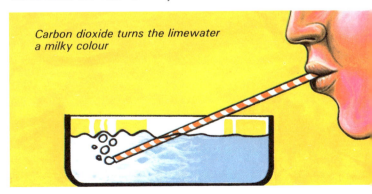

Carbon dioxide turns the limewater a milky colour

Carbon dioxide is an important gas needed by green plants and trees for making food in their leaves. Green leaves are like little factories and use carbon dioxide to make sugar. All natural water has carbon dioxide in it, too, which keeps water plants alive. Animal life is dependent on green plants for survival, so without carbon dioxide gas, life as we know it would perish.

When carbon or anything containing carbon is burned in a good supply of air, carbon dioxide is formed. The coal and oil we burn in factories and our homes makes hundreds of cubic metres of carbon dioxide, which joins the air when it is discharged through tall chimneys.

Carbon dioxide gas is heavier than air, and will sink to the bottom of any container you make it in. Scientists have worked out that it is 1.5 times heavier than air.

Pour a little vinegar into a plastic bag and add some baking soda to make carbon dioxide. Squeeze the mouth of the bag tightly shut. What happens?

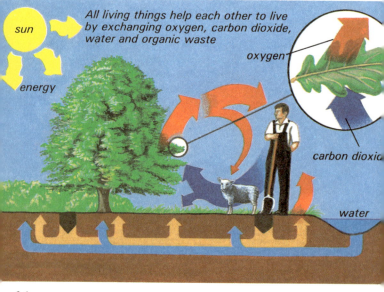

sun

energy

All living things help each other to live by exchanging oxygen, carbon dioxide, water and organic waste

oxygen

carbon dioxi

water

Try this experiment.

Put a teaspoonful of baking soda in a dry jam jar and pour in about ten drops of vinegar. When the baking soda is bubbling and giving off carbon dioxide, carefully put a lighted taper into the bubbling pot. What happens?

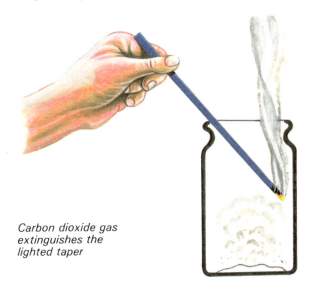

Carbon dioxide gas extinguishes the lighted taper

The flame goes out because of the carbon dioxide coming from the fizzing baking soda. Carbon dioxide gas puts out flames. Some fire extinguishers operate by forcing jets of carbon dioxide foam through a nozzle onto flames.

Lemonade contains a solution of carbon dioxide in water, but since it is dissolved under pressure, much of it escapes when the lemonade bottle top is unscrewed. Pour some lemonade into a glass and look carefully through a magnifying glass at where the bubbles form. Do they form just anywhere? Do they appear as large bubbles? What happens if you tap the glass with a pencil?

Hard water

As rain water falls through the air it collects and dissolves a little carbon dioxide. When the rain hits the ground, it trickles into the soil, and if there is any limestone or chalk in the earth, it joins with the water to produce hard water. Hard water does not mix well with soap and it is difficult to wash clothes and get them clean in hard water. It also coats kettles and washing machines with a hard, furry-looking substance known as *lime scale*. It is good for drinking, though, and does us no harm.

Beachy Head shows the vast layer of chalk which lies beneath the earth in some parts of the country

Many homes have water softeners which work in a simple way. The house water flows through a vessel containing a coarse powder called Zeolite. This, together with salt, acts as a water softener.

Is your house water hard or soft? Look inside your kettle. If there is a lot of lime scale you are probably living in a hard water area.

Dissolving

Many people sweeten tea and coffee by adding a spoonful of sugar. When the drink is stirred, the sugar disappears. We say it has *dissolved* in the hot liquid.

It is important for chemists to find out whether substances will or will not dissolve in water. They find this a helpful way of identifying unknown substances because some chemicals dissolve easily, others not at all.

Find out which kitchen substances dissolve in water.

Things you need:
¼ teaspoonful each of sugar, curry powder, table salt, baking soda and chalk
   (crush a stick of chalk until it is a fine powder)
5 small, empty jars with lids

What you do:
(1) After labelling the jars 1 to 5, half fill each one with water.
(2) Add a different substance to each jar. Put on the lids and shake each jar twenty times.
(3) Take off the lids and see which powders have dissolved. (You can keep the jar with table salt in it for the next experiment.)

When a substance dissolves in liquid we say it is *soluble*. When it does not dissolve it is *insoluble*. Is sand soluble in water? Try some experiments of your own and keep a record of soluble and insoluble substances.

Evaporation

Take the jar in which you dissolved table salt and drain off 2 teaspoonfuls of the liquid onto a clean saucer. Leave the saucer in a warm place, such as a windowsill, for a few days. The water will eventually evaporate leaving behind the salt in the form of crystals.

Salt panning in West Africa

Solutions

Sea-water covers about two-thirds of our planet and is a good example of a *solution* because there are many salts dissolved in it. A solution is the blending of two or more substances. If you put a small amount of salt into a cup of water, you get a weak or *dilute* solution. Add more salt and the solution gets stronger or more *concentrated*, as chemists say. The salt is called the *solute*, the water is the *solvent*. Sea-water is a concentrated solution because rain, through countless years, has been collecting salt from underground rocks and depositing it into the sea.

Find out how to make a solution of salt.

Things you will need:

salt   spoon
cup   magnifying glass
water   drinking glass

What you do:

(1) Drop a *pinch* of salt into ⅓ cup of warm water and stir it in. You now have a dilute salt solution.

(2) Add a *spoonful* of salt and stir, and the solution is now a concentrated one.

(3) Pour some of the concentrated salt solution into a drinking glass and hold it up to the light. Can you see any particles of salt floating in the water? Try looking through a magnifying glass for floating particles.

There are rules that solutions always obey

(1) The solute cannot be seen, even with a magnifying glass.

(2) Solutions cannot be filtered, because the particles are very small.

(3) They are always transparent.

(4) The solute never falls to the bottom of the glass.

Mixtures

Not every substance will dissolve or follow the rules for a solution. When particles do not dissolve this is called a *mixture*. Which of the following are mixtures and which are solutions?

sugar and water   *ink and water*
sand and water   *pepper and water*

Add each substance to be tested to a jar of cold water and stir. Does the sand disappear? Can you see it with a magnifying glass. Is it a solution? List the solutions and mixtures in your notebook. Can you discover more mixtures and solutions?

Sand and water

Ink and water

Unsaturated, saturated and supersaturated solutions

If we squeeze a sponge under water, then release the pressure, the sponge fills with water. Lift the sponge out and water drips from it. The sponge is *saturated*. Chemists use this word in a similar way when they talk about solutions they work with in their laboratories.

Sugar crystals

A tablespoonful of sugar in a glass of cold water is called a *dilute* or *unsaturated* solution of sugar. If you keep on adding sugar until no more will dissolve, you would have a saturated solution. This means that the water is holding, *in solution*, as much as it can. If an extra pinch of sugar is added, some falls to the bottom.

A solution that contains more sugar than can normally be dissolved is called a *supersaturated* solution. Gently heat a cupful of water in a saucepan (take care!) Pour it into another saucepan and saturate it with sugar. Because the temperature of the water is high, the water will dissolve more sugar than it normally would.

Let the solution cool and then add another pinch of sugar. The extra sugar will act as *seed crystals* and the dissolved sugar will grow around it.

Desert chemistry

In a desert in Arizona, USA, there is a famous National Park called the *Petrified Forest*. Here there are great logs of beautiful minerals called jasper and agate.

Petrified wood is manufactured by nature in a special way. The mineralised logs were once living trees in a prehistoric forest. When they fell to the ground, they were covered, before they could decay, by sand, mud and volcanic ash. Eventually a geological upheaval lifted the land, and millions of years of wind and rain exposed the trees. But they had changed — the wood had been replaced by coloured minerals. The trees are now solid rock.

Crystals in nature

Nature is perhaps the best chemist, and certainly grows the most beautiful and spectacular crystals. Minerals in the ground form crystals when conditions are right. There are many different crystal shapes and colours, some so delicate and perfect that they seem to have been made by expert craftsmen.

The word *crystal* comes from the Greek, *krystallos*, which means icy cold. It was once thought that crystals were water, frozen so hard that it would never melt. Some countries are famous for certain types of crystal, such as Brazil for its magnificent amethysts and South Africa for diamonds.

The best crystals are formed in rock cavities. Water movement on and in the earth's crust mixes minerals together in the ground. The fierce heat at the earth's centre forces molten rock towards the surface. The minerals in the molten rock are left behind when evaporation takes place, and crystals develop. The slower the evaporation of the water, the larger the crystals will be. This process is happening all the time.

above *A petrified log in the National Park, Arizona, USA*

below *Some of the earth's natural crystals*

Growing crystals

Before you try growing crystals of your own, look at some sugar and table salt through a magnifying glass. What do you notice about the shape of their crystals?

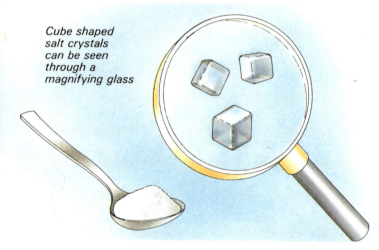

Cube shaped salt crystals can be seen through a magnifying glass

You can grow crystals at home, using the same method as occurs in nature. Growing crystals will give you hours of pleasure and delight. You need patience, though, because crystals grow slowly. The longer you wait the better the result.

Things you need:
4 clean jam jars
14 g table salt
14 g sugar
14 g cream of tartar $\Big\}$ Obtainable from a chemist
14 g alum
nylon thread
water
old saucepan
old saucers

What you do:

The following recipe can be used for all the substances in the list but it is a good idea to grow *alum* crystals first because they grow fastest.

(1) Make four tops for the jam jars. Turn one jar upside down on a sheet of cardboard, carefully draw a circle round the mouth, and then cut out the circular disc. The disc you have made will fit over the top of the jar without falling in. Repeat this for the other jars. Pierce two small holes in each disc.

(2) Gently heat 75 ml of water in the old saucepan and add 14 g of alum. Stir until all the alum has disappeared.

(3) Take the pan off the heat and let the solution cool down. Pour a little onto a saucer and save the rest of the solution in one of the jam jars. Wash out your saucepan.

(4) Drop a single alum crystal into the saucer and leave it on a windowsill overnight. The next day there will be clusters of tiny alum crystals in the bottom of the saucer. Look at them with a magnifying glass. What shape are they?

Alum crystals produced by evaporation

(5) Choose the biggest and best shaped crystal. Tie a length of nylon thread to it. This seed crystal is going to form the base for new crystal growth in the jam jars.

(6) Pour the solution you saved in the jam jar back into the saucepan and gently heat this again until any crystals have dissolved (some crystals will have formed in the jar overnight).

(7) Let this cool again. Pour it back into your jar and wash out the saucepan.

(8) Tie the seed crystal to the cardboard disc and hang it so that the crystal is suspended in the solution (see diagram). Leave it somewhere cool and safe for a few days.

(9) The suspended crystal will grow into a bigger, more beautiful alum crystal. If you want to increase its size, then make another solution and repeat the experiment.

A crystal garden

The salts of most metals combine with a substance called sodium silicate. Sodium silicate dissolves in water to form a solution known as water glass. It is used to preserve eggs and you can buy it from a chemist's shop.

DANGER: You can grow the most beautiful crystal garden but you will need to buy substances from the chemist *which should NEVER be put in your mouth. ALWAYS* wash your hands after touching these crystals. Follow these instructions carefully.

To make a crystal garden you need:
water glass
(or egg preserver)
a large jam jar
some crystals of ferrous sulphate, copper sulphate and iron alum (you can buy these from the chemist in small quantities, but they must not be put into your mouth)
washed sand

What you do:

(1) Half fill the jar with water glass and fill it to the top with cold tap water.

(2) Put in a layer of washed sand about 1 cm thick at the bottom of the jar, and drop in the crystals one at a time.

(3) They will begin to produce lots of tiny crystals that grow towards the surface of the water, forming a beautiful crystal garden of different coloured crystals. Be patient for the best results!

This 'forest' grew in only 5 minutes

Acids and alkalis

Acids and alkalis are important chemical substances. All acids taste sour. The word *acid* comes from the Latin, *acidus*, which means sour. Hundreds of acids occur in the natural world, even in our gardens. Unripe fruits taste sour because they contain acid. For instance, unripe apples contain *malic acid* and grapes contain *tartaric acid*. Lemons contain *citric acid* which is why fruits such as lemons and limes are called citrus fruits.

Most acids are harmless but some are very dangerous. Sulphuric acid, hydrochloric acid and nitric acid are all very harmful and, if touched, will destroy your skin. All three, though, are used by chemists in the manufacture of fertilisers and plastics.

The word *alkali* is Arabic and means *ashes*. Alkalis are made from burning wood and some kinds of seashore plants. They have a bitter taste and feel soapy when rubbed between your fingers. Vast areas of desert in the USA are alkaline regions where few plants grow and little animal life can survive. Sodium hydroxide, also known as caustic soda, is a well known but very dangerous alkali. It destroys human skin and clothing very quickly.

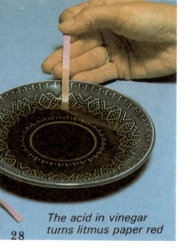

The acid in vinegar turns litmus paper red

Chemists use a specially treated paper called *litmus paper* when they test unknown liquids to check if they are acids or alkalis. Litmus is a dye made from plants. It is *neutral*, which means it contains neither acid or alkali. When it is dipped into *acids* it turns *red*, and it turns *blue* when in contact with *alkalis*. Chemists call litmus paper an *indicator*. You can make an indicator to identify acids and alkalis in your kitchen.

Things you need:

half a fresh red cabbage, coffee, water, orange squash, toothpaste, earth, vinegar, tea, scouring powder (e.g., Vim or Ajax), two plastic bowls, old saucers

What you do:

(1) Cut the red cabbage into thin strips and put these into a bowl.

(2) Boil a kettle and very carefully pour some hot water into the bowl. The juice from the cabbage will colour the water a darkish purple. Let the solution cool and strain the liquid into a plastic bowl. Throw away the cabbage.

(3) Make a solution or mixture of each of the substances in the list and pour some of each one into a different saucer.

(4) Using a straw as a dropper, drip a couple of drops of cabbage water onto each solution in turn. What happens? Which substances are acid?

The saliva in your mouth may be acid or alkali. Test it and see and then test the saliva of other members of your family to see any differences.

Dyes

Picking blackberries is a messy job. Your fingers get stained with blackberry juice. Early man discovered how to change the colour of his clothes with berry juice, and gradually developed the art of *dyeing*.

Nowadays chemists make dyes for us, but until the middle of the 19th century, all dyes were made from plants, animals, and minerals found in the ground. A long time ago, the Phoenicians crushed and boiled murex sea shells to make purple dye. The word *Phoenician* comes from a Greek word for purple. Their *Tyrian* purple was special because it took 8,500 shells to make one gram of dye! Roman Emperors wore Tyrian purple as a sign of high rank.

Black dye was made from oak galls. The gall is not a tree fruit. It develops when gall wasps lay their eggs on oak trees. The larvae wriggle inside the branches and develop the woody galls. By boiling galls in water, monks extracted a strong, black dye which they used as ink for writing their manuscripts.

Part of an old manuscript known as the Book of Kells

A Roman Emperor in Tyrian purple

Dyes were very important in the textile industries in Yorkshire and Lancashire during the Industrial Revolution in the late 18th century. Certain areas became associated with particular colours. Green baize and red flannel from Manchester and Huddersfield were exported to America. The Navajo Indians in America were expert weavers but could not make a good red dye, so they used Yorkshire red flannel and rewove it into rugs and blankets.

In 1856, at the Royal College of Chemistry in London, William Perkins made an artificial mauve colour dye from coal tar, and within three years, other chemists added a great range of man-made colour dyes, all from coal tar.

Mordants

Some natural and man-made dyes do not give good permanent colours unless another chemical is used when the cloth is boiled. These chemicals are called *mordants* and they make the dye *bite* into the cloth. Urine, tree bark and wood ash have been used as mordants to produce lasting colours, but today, we can buy man-made mordants from chemist shops.

Dyes and dyeing

Dyeing takes patience, care and time; set aside an afternoon and a morning for this chemistry experiment.

Things you need:

water

60 g alum

1 tablespoonful cream of tartar

30 g onion skins

sieve

white handkerchief or piece of white cotton cloth

2 large saucepans (enamel or stainless steel)

jam jar

cloth

What you do:

(1) Dissolve the alum and cream of tartar in 500 ml of warm water in the jar and add this mixture to a large pan of cold water.

(2) Put the handkerchief or cloth into the pan and gradually heat, stirring all the time. This will mordant the material.

(3) Simmer gently for an hour and then switch off the heat and allow the water to cool.

(4) Spread the onion skins on to a chopping board and cut them into very small pieces. Put them into a small container full of water and soak them overnight.

(5) On the second day, boil the onion skins and simmer for an hour. Then strain the liquid into another large pan, leaving the skins behind in the sieve.

This piece of cloth was dyed in the onion skin liquid

(6) Add enough warm water to the liquid in the pan to cover the handkerchief or cloth.

(7) Add the mordanted cloth and bring to the boil. Simmer gently for one hour. Take the pan off the heat and leave to cool slightly.

(8) Carefully remove the cloth from the pan, using a pair of tongs, and wash it in soapy water. Rinse the handkerchief or cloth until the water runs clear.

What colour have you dyed your cloth? Now experiment with other substances. Dyes can be made in this way from many things, including tea leaves, pine cones and red cabbage. See what colours you produce and make notes of quantities in your notebook each time you make a new colour.

Cold-water dyes are easy to make, but they will not stay in cloth. It's fun to make some, though, from such things as earth, coal dust, or anything that stains, and to use them as paints for your next water-colour picture.

33

Paper and paint

Chemistry helps in the production of paper and paint. It is thought that paper was first used by the Chinese, and the idea soon spread to other parts of the world. In 1490, the first paper mill in England was opened in Stevenage, a town in Hertfordshire.

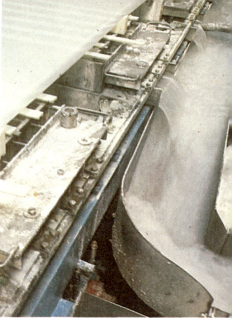

Wet end of a paper machine showing pulp

If you rip a sheet of paper and look closely with a magnifying glass at the torn edges, you can see fine hair-like fibres of *cellulose*, the substance from which the cell-walls of plants and trees are made. When paper is

Reel-up on a paper machine

produced, wood is broken down until every fibre is separated and the *pulp* is then mixed with water.

Paper was made by hand until early in the 19th century. Most paper today is made in huge paper-making machines, from wood pulp or other vegetable fibre. The pulp is boiled in chemicals and then bleached (if it is going to be white), dried and cut into sheets.

Paint making began when Stone Age man used 'earth colours' to make his cave paintings. Today, chemists use natural and man-made substances to produce paint. One recent development discovered by chemists is latex emulsion paint which contains man-made rubber. This paint is very easy to use and is long-lasting: ideal for the home decorator.

Making nettle paper

You can make paper from common stinging nettles.

Things you need:

lots of nettle leaves   old large saucepan
pair of big scissors   plastic bucket
sieve   pair of gardening gloves
newspapers

What you do:

(1) Put on the pair of gardening gloves and strip about 50 leaves off some stinging nettle plants.

(2) Cut them into small pieces and soak them in a bucket of cold water for two or three days.

(3) Drain off the water and tip the leaves into a saucepan, half full of water. Boil the cut leaves until the water turns a straw colour.

(4) Let the water cool and drain the leaves into a sink.

(5) Scoop out the leaves with the sieve and spread them out carefully.

(6) The fibres of the nettle leaves bind together, leaving a sheet of thick, yellowy 'paper'.

(7) Rest the damp paper between sheets of newspaper and press with two or three heavy books. Remove your hand-made sheet of paper after two days.

Separating colours

As well as producing new colours for the clothing industry, chemists also investigate coloured liquids. Colours are not always pure. They are often several colours mixed together. Have you noticed that if a page of your writing gets wet, the ink or felt pen colour runs and spreads across the page, separating into different colours?

Let's find out how to separate colours.

Things you need:

several yogurt pots   drinking straws
felt-tipped pens   food colouring
kitchen roll or blotting paper

What you do:

(1) Cut several strips of kitchen roll about 10 cm by 10 cm and cut a narrow strip down to the centre of each one. Bend the strip back and put it into a pot half full of water. (See diagram.)

(2) Use a straw dropper to drop a blob of food colouring onto the centre of each paper. What happens?

The water rises up the strip to the colour and after a while separates the blob into different colours. What colours do you get from red food colouring? Can you split up the ink colours of felt pens?

Filtering liquids

Chemists have to separate fine particles of solids which are floating or mixed in liquids. If the particles are so small that they would slip through a kitchen sieve, chemists use *filter paper* to clean liquids. What happens on a bigger scale? All our domestic water needs purifying so the chemists have devised a way of filtering out the impurities. At the Water Works, water is passed through huge layers of sand and gravel called *filter-beds*. This cleans the water.

Try it for yourself and see how it works.

(1) Put some sand and gravel in layers in the top of a funnel.

(2) Make a muddy mixture of soil and water and pour this into the top of the funnel and collect the water in a jar. Is the water clear? Does your filtering system work?

(3) What happens if you pour through some cold coffee or tea? Can you use this method for straining solutions?

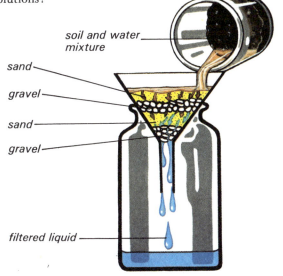

soil and water mixture

sand

gravel

sand

gravel

filtered liquid

Rust

Rust is a problem. Iron and steel develop brownish red patches of rust when they are unprotected and exposed to damp air. Some chemical fumes from factory chimneys can also cause metals to rust.

Rust is a chemical change called *oxidation*. It happens when metal and oxygen combine. First a small blob appears on the metal which gets bigger and flakes off, leaving a new surface to be attacked. Iron bridges have been known to weaken and collapse through the effects of rust and we often see patches of rust on old cars.

The metal can be protected against attack from rust by coating it with paint, oil, or some non-rusting metals. The metal, *chromium*, does not rust and car bumpers, headlights, and our bathroom fittings are protected by chromium plating. Tin is another non-rusting metal and is used in the canning industry. Nowadays, plastic is often used instead of metals because this will not be attacked by oxygen and water.

Let's find out how to prevent rust.

Things you need:

jam jars   Vaseline
house paint   9 shiny iron nails
cooking oil

To discover which conditions are best for rust, make sure you choose different kinds of places to set up your experiments. In the warmest, coldest, lightest and darkest places in your home, put a jar with a shiny nail inside. Check after a few days. Which jar has the rustiest nail?

(1) When you have found the best rust-growing place, get four jars. In the first jar, put a dry shiny nail.

(2) In the second jar, put a nail covered with paint.

(3) In the third jar, put a nail covered in Vaseline grease.

(4) In the last jar, put a nail dipped in oil.

(5) Put all the jars in the best rust growing position and leave them for a few days. What happens?

(6) Now put a nail into a jar of boiled water, with half the nail sticking out of the water. Which half rusts? Why does only half the nail rust?

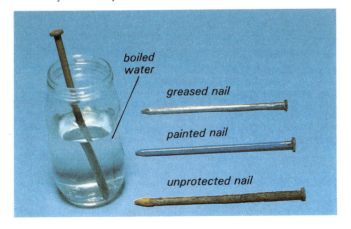

boiled water

greased nail

painted nail

unprotected nail

The chemistry of cooking

When one is cooking, chemistry helps. Without certain ingredients to create a chemical change, many recipes would not work.

If you try to make bread without *yeast*, it wouldn't *rise*. You would produce hard, flat bread. Yeast is a tiny fungus which grows by developing small buds to form new plants. As the yeast grows it gives off carbon dioxide which forms little gas pockets in the dough. To start this process the dough must be worked well with the hands. This is called *kneading* and must be done for at least ten minutes.

Sugar feeds yeast and quickens the growing process. Salt slows down the yeast growth but makes bread taste better. The salt is therefore mixed with the flour so that it does not come into direct contact with the yeast.

A loaf before and after baking which shows the effect of yeast

Let's experiment with yeast and watch how sugar reacts with it.

Things you need:

sugar	dried yeast
balloon	bottle
jam jar	teaspoon
limewater	

What you do:

(1) Half fill a jam jar with warm tap water and add five teaspoonfuls of sugar.

(2) Stir until the sugar dissolves.

(3) Pour the solution into a clean bottle and wash the empty jar.

(4) Mix one teaspoonful of yeast and two teaspoonfuls of water in the jar and carefully pour this into the bottle.

(5) Fix a balloon tightly to the neck of the bottle, tying it round and round with string so that it can't blow off. Put it in a warm place.

The yeast gives off carbon dioxide gas which inflates the balloon

41

The carbon dioxide turns the limewater a milky colour

After a while the solution will begin to bubble and slowly the balloon will be blown up by gas made by the yeast acting on the sugar. Carefully pinch the neck so that the gas doesn't escape and remove the balloon. With the neck of the balloon under the surface of a jar of limewater, let the gas escape. What happens? (Don't forget to wash your hands.)

Baking powder acts in the same way as yeast by giving off carbon dioxide when mixed with water and heated. Plain flour, margarine, sugar, eggs and milk combine to make a cake but you must add baking powder if the cake is to be light and fluffy. Self-raising flour already contains baking powder or a similar substance to make cakes rise.

Cream of tartar is sometimes used for making scones because it too helps the mixture to rise. Yeast, baking powder and cream of tartar are all known as *raising agents*. Cream of tartar is a fine white powder obtained from the bottom of wine storage barrels and casks. The powder develops from fermenting grape juice which contains tartaric acid.

When some fruits and vegetables are cut and exposed to the air, they turn a dark, unattractive colour. Bananas, apples and potatoes do this. Chefs use lemon juice to prevent this discolouration. As soon as the food is cut, squeeze the juice over and the citric acid in lemons does the trick.

Another acid used by cooks is vinegar, which is used to preserve food from deterioration. The word vinegar comes from the French, *vin aigre*, meaning sour wine. Food stored in vinegar is *pickled* and onions, cucumbers, cabbage and beetroot are the most common ones. The vinegar stops the food from turning rotten and also gives a very characteristic flavour.

There are two groups of vinegars: malt vinegars which are made from beer, and wine vinegars, made from grape and other fruit juices. Both are produced by the action of bacteria on the wine or beer.

Many years ago, before refrigerators had been invented, it was very difficult to keep meat fresh for more than a day or two. Joints of meat, bacon and fish were salted to preserve them for eating at a later date. The bacteria which turns food bad cannot reproduce in salt and so travellers often took salted meat with them on long journeys.

Housewives also used to smoke their meat and fish in the fireplace, because smoking also preserves food by killing off the bacteria which would affect the food.

Let's experiment with cooking by making some American baking powder biscuits.

Things you need:

225 g plain flour	mixing bowl
110 g margarine	rolling pin
90 ml (3 fl oz) milk	knife
10 g baking powder	board
5 g salt	pastry cutter
	baking sheet
	fork

Turn on the oven at gas mark 7 (electric 220C/425F)

What you do:

(1) Divide each of the ingredients into two equal parts. Use the first group to make the baking powder biscuits as given below.

(2) Put the flour, all 10 g of baking powder and salt into a mixing bowl and mix them together well.

(3) Add the fats in small pieces and rub with your finger tips until the mixture looks like small bread crumbs.

(4) Add some milk until the mixture forms a soft doughball.

soft doughball

(5) Cover a board with flour, and also your hands and the rolling pin.

(6) First knead the dough gently until it is smooth.

(7) Now use the floured rolling pin to roll the dough until it is 2 cm thick.

(8) Cut out the scones, using a pastry cutter, and prick each one with a fork. Place them on an ungreased baking sheet and bake in the oven for 12 to 15 minutes.

(9) While these scones are in the oven, clear away and make another batch, using the other half of the ingredients, but this time leave out the baking powder.

(10) When both batches are baked, compare them and see what difference the baking powder made to the first group. Which group look like scones: the ones with or without the raising agent?

The Americans call our scones, "biscuits", and our biscuits, "cookies". You have made scones but your second group probably look like English biscuits because they had no raising agent.

without
baking powder

with
baking powder

The starch in the potato turns the iodine black

The starch test

Many foods that we eat each day contain *starch*, a sugar-like substance that people on diets want to avoid. You can easily test foods to see if they contain starch.

Things you need:

bread
carrot
raw meat
slice of potato
apple
dried white rice

old saucers
straw dropper
tincture of iodine
   (obtainable from
   the chemist)
jam jar
plastic spoon

What you do:

(1) Make a solution of the iodine by adding 5 drops of iodine to the jam jar and pouring in cold water until it is 6 cm deep. Stir well.

(2) Put the potato on a saucer and drip onto it 2 or 3 drops of iodine solution. Watch the potato turn bluey black. Iodine is an indicator for the presence of starch. Now test all the other foods you have collected and see what happens.

Mouldy food

Keeping food fresh is a problem. In damp, moist conditions much of our food goes mouldy if it is not protected. Moulds are tiny plants called fungi, and their minute *spores* (seeds) are in the air we breathe. Moulds are easy to grow. Let's find out how to grow them.

Things you need:

washing-up liquid bottles
polythene bags
a slice of cheese
orange peel
a piece of old leather
a scrap of plastic

cotton wool
elastic bands
a slice of apple
bread
some small stones

What you do:

(1) First you need to make mould growers from the washing-up liquid bottles. With scissors, carefully cut round the top part of each bottle. Turn the top upside down to form a funnel and place it in the bottom section (see diagram). Fill the bottom part with water.

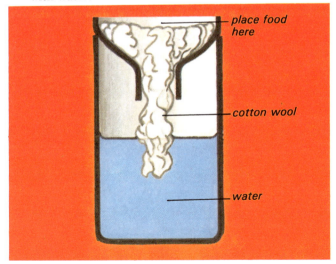

place food here

cotton wool

water

(2) Put some cotton wool in each funnel and pull it through the spout. Place the funnel back on the base and make sure that the cotton wool touches the water and is soaked.

(3) Put different food in each mould grower, cover it with a polythene bag and place it on a window sill. Check each day to see what is happening and record this in your notebook.

Which foods grow moulds? Are the moulds a different colour? Which food grew mould first? Now put the leather, some stones and the plastic in different containers and see what happens.

Moulds only grow on things that have once lived. Such materials are called *organic*. Things which have never lived are called *inorganic*. A stone, which is inorganic, does not give mould spores anything to feed on.

Did the orange peel grow a blue mould? This is *penicillin*. Penicillin is used as a medicine. Sir Alexander Fleming (1881-1955) discovered this by accident. He left a dish of bacteria uncovered and later found that it had mould on it. The bacteria round the mould had died and from this observation Fleming, in 1928, discovered the drug that has since saved thousands of lives.

Mould on bread

Sterilisation

Louis Pasteur (1822-1895) was a French chemist who was fascinated by moulds. He developed a method, known as *pasteurisation*, to make milk safe to drink by removing harmful bacteria. He did this by heating the liquid and this killed the germs. Hospitals *sterilise* instruments and dressings to prevent infection spreading, by heating them in special containers called *autoclaves*.

A commercial autoclave which sterilises dressings before they leave the factory

Chemistry in the garden

Garden soil is normally fertile enough for growing vegetables and flowers. Vegetables are greedy feeders and take a lot of goodness from the soil as they grow. Each time a gardener uses the soil he or she should put back the goodness for the next crop. This is done by treating the soil or "digging in" with animal manure, man-made fertilisers or organic compost.

Fertilisers provide chemical substances that are necessary for good plant growth. There are four chemical substances which are very important for the garden.

Nitrogen makes plants grow as big as possible. Plants that grow in ground which is short of nitrogen are stunted and often yellow in colour.

Potash promotes the health and vigour of plants, helps disease resistance, and maintains the colour of their leaves and flowers.

Phosphorus encourages the growth of good fruit and flowers.

Lime maintains the acid/alkali balance in the soil so that plant food, in solution, can be absorbed through the root hairs of the plants. You could test whether soil is acid or alkali, by using the indicator described on page 29. Also, very alkaline soils will fizz when tested with vinegar.

Crop spraying

A compost heap

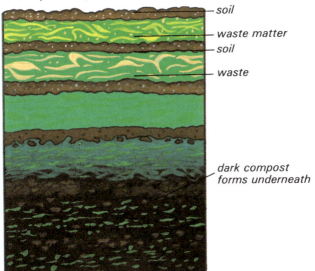

— soil
— waste matter
— soil
— waste

dark compost forms underneath

Chemists have developed many different kinds of fertilisers to help the gardener and the farmer. Next time you visit a garden centre, look at the different chemicals on display.

Many people prefer to use natural plant food made by slowly rotting vegetable waste, table scraps, and grass cuttings in a compost heap. The waste scraps are piled high and sprinkled with soil at intervals. The heap gets warm as it gets bigger, due to the action of the bacteria which causes the materials to rot down to a dark compost. Farmers also spread rotting manure on their fields.

Chemists make liquid fertilisers for houseplants. These are concentrated and need to be diluted with water before use. They contain all the chemicals that plants need and act very quickly. As their effect is not long lasting, liquid fertilisers need to be fed to plants regularly during the growing season.

INDEX